TREET POETRY.

. A. HEDLEY.

The word guy)

FIRST PUBLICATION OF A COLLECTION OF MY NEW POETRY, PLUS A
ENEROUS SPRINKLING OF MY BEST-KNOWN AWARD/COMPETITION-
VINNING POETRY.

mix of romance and nostalgia, with a lyrical, rhythmic, slant.

thought...

ove books of all kinds...

ne next time that you buy someone a gift, chocolates and flowers are the most
ommon of gifts, so they say. Think outside the box and consider a book, most
ooks cost around the same price as flowers or chocolates, but they won't wilt,
nd they won't make you put on weight. They can however last a lifetime, and
ou will always remember who gifted that book to you.

INTRO.

What is 'Street poetry' and who am I?
I was brought up on the backstreets of Tyneside, a working-class area where any sign of weakness or non-conformity was frowned upon. In my early teens I discovered my love of words, and most of all my ability to quickly marry lyrics to music, which was OK, acceptable if you like. However, to say I was writing poetry would not have sat well with my streetwise friends, not at all like the world we live in today. So, under my guise as a lyric writer everything in the garden was rosy, and I somehow got tagged with the name of 'The word guy' in some circles
At around that time, I began to write romantic poetry, nostalgic poetry, even some political poetry, however, most of my poetry was observational and still carried a rhythmic slant, which is still evident in most of my work today.
One day, a close friend of mine turned up unexpectedly, I was sitting writing at my mother's living room table behind a pile of finished poetry, of course he started to pick up and read various poems, and one poem where I had penned a tearful breakup with my ex-girlfriend. He looked sideways at me and said, 'I hope one of your sisters wrote this' for some unknown reason I replied angrily, 'You know nothing, that's 'street poetry' born from these very streets we walk today
He replied, 'I knew that.'
In my early twenties I moved to Scotland to work in the oil industry, I still live in Scotland today. In my spare time I would write short stories and poetry for the local press.
About a decade ago I returned to my writing in earnest.
I have now had a trilogy of private detective novels published to great acclaim, and seven very popular poetry books.
The majority of my books are FOUR or FIVE-STAR RATED.
My f/c page 'About my detective novels and more' which also highlights my poetry, has many thousands of followers.

WELCOME AND ENJOY.
A. A. HEDLEY.

CONTENTS.

26. CLUB CAVERNA.
27. DANCING WITH RAINDROPS.
28. YOUR SMILE.
29. MIDNIGHT'S STREET.
30. WHY.
31. THROUGH MIDNIGHT.
32. WRITING ON WATER.
33. WHEN YOU RETURN.
34. FAREWELL.
35. BROKEN MIRROR.
36. BLACK AND WHITE STREETS.
37. ORDINARY JOE.
38. ANGELINA.
39. RAIN IN MY HEART.
40. OLD ROBERT.
41. BLUE SKIES.
42. THE ROAD TO DON'T KNOW WHERE.
43. ROSE IN THE SNOW.
44. WALKING WITH THE CLOUDS.
45. LETTING GO.
46. REGRETS.
47. HOMECOMING.
48. CHILLED ROMANCE.
49. FOREST OF LOVE.
50. END OF SHOW.

76. GIRL ON A BEACH.
77. FIRST DATE THOUGHTS.
78. YOU LEFT ME BABE.
79. SPRINGTIME.
80. JUST FLY.
81. SHE.
82. YOU.
83. WHAT IF.
84. ANOTHER DAY.
85. THE PAPER CINEMA.
86. STREET LIFE.
87. AWAKENING.
88. THE PALLY IS CLOSED.
89. OLD LADY.
90. POETIC IMAGES.
91. THE AVENUE.
92. ALONE AGAIN.
93. THE GHOST OF BARLEEZE.
94. THE DOG THAT NEVER WAS.
95. HERSHWHIN COOP.
96. THE CITY.
97. PINSTRIPE PUPPET.
98. LOVING YOU.
99. MERRY CHRISTMAS.
100. MY SECRET VALENTINE.

101. HAPPY STREET.
102. DREAMY RAINBOW LAND.
103. NIGHT OF DAY.
104. SUMMER ROMANCE.
105. LIVING IN A DREAM.
106. MY YOUNG FRIEND.
107. FLOWERS TO A FALLEN FRIEND.
108. SLEEPY VALENTINE.
109. THE OLD DANCER.
110. ALL ALONE AT CHRISTMAS.
111. THE ONLY GIRL FOR ME.
112. DANCING IN THE DARK.
113. ONCE AGAIN.
114. LADY.
115. A TEXT GOODBYE.
116. VELVET DREAMS.
117. LOVES EMBERS.
118. SEA OF LOVE.
119. WHISPERED STARLIGHT.
120. DECLARATION OF LOVE.
121. DREAMS.
122. FREESCAPE.
123. AHA.
124. SHIFTING SANDS.
125. SEASONS.

1.

MISS YOU.

Can’t hear your voice,
Footsteps are gone,
No sweet perfume,
Which once was here, in every room.
I dine alone,
One cup not two,
I should have never said,
The words, that we were through.

I miss you so,
I love you still,
I loved you long before we met,
And always will.

Sweet girl of mine,
Where are you now,
Maybe a loving breeze,
Can guide you back, somehow.

Can’t hear your voice,
Footsteps are gone,
No sweet perfume,
Which once was here, in every room.
I dine alone,
One cup not two,
I should have never said,
The words, that we were through.

2.

PICTURES.
I look at pictures every day,
A picture needs no words to say.
For it speaks to tell you all it needs,
Through the shadows of the darkened trees,
Just as the eyes, of a portrait,
Throw a glance, to enhance,
All those thoughts, within you.

As the waves upon the sea,
Show the way that life must be.
Some days they're calm and seem, so peaceful,
But never trust them as, they're deceitful,
For their mood swings,
Throw an anger, to the winds,
They meet each day,
And they will play, to taunt you.

So, with every picture you have seen,
You should recall how life has been.
A rollercoaster full, of highs and lows,
A busy street that's full, of stops and goes,
So, as a web love, and a web of lies,
Paint so many skies, you realise,
That all the clouds,
Are moving.

I look at pictures every day,
A picture needs no words to say.
For it speaks to tell you all it needs,
Through the shadows of the darkened trees,
Just as the eyes, of a portrait,
Throw a glance, to enhance, all those thoughts, within you.

3.

WASHED OUT.

I've been walking in the driving rain,
Will I ever see your face again?
As the raindrops, from the streetlights,
Catch the tears, within my eyes,
I realise,
I've lost you.

And now with every step I take,
I hear it echo each mistake,
Reminding me, about the things I said,
When I could have said, nice things instead.
Now I'm sitting, on a park bench,
Drenched right through, because of you,
And all the ways,
I messed up.

As I gaze up through the driving rain,
I only wish that you could feel my pain,
Then you would know, despite my selfish ways,
You'd be amazed, to see how much,
I love you.

I've been walking in the driving rain,
Will I ever see your face again?
As the raindrops, from the streetlights,
Catch the tears, within my eyes,
I realise,
I've lost you.

4.

DON'T SEND ME FLOWERS.

Don't send me flowers, when I'm crying,
When it was you who sent my tears,
Don't smile at me, when I am dying,
After lying all these years.

Don't hold me tight, and say you love me,
Don't kiss my lips, and say you're mine,
Don't gaze into, my tired eyes dear,
And tell me everything is fine.

You know, I know there is another,
You've tried to hide throughout the years,
Don't send me flowers, when I'm crying,
For they can't take away my tears.

5.

ANOTHER WET MONDAY.

Another wet Monday,
With nothing to do,
It's six weeks past, since I lost my job,
And then I lost you.

And your new guy,
They say, he treats you bad,
I was so good to you,
And, that makes me sad.

I'm still here girl,
Dreaming of you,
I can't believe, that you walked out,
Leaving me so blue.

Make my wet Monday,
Dry up and shine,
Just make my phone ring,
And say you're mine.

Or is this just, another wet Monday,
With nothing to do,
Just to mope around, without a sound,
Dreaming of you,
On yet another wet Monday.

6.

JUST WALKING IN THE RAIN.

I am just walking in the rain,
Watching the breeze dance in the trees,
And I'm whistling a tune,
Just whistling a tune.

The rain is going pitter-pat,
And there is nothing wrong with that,
I am just walking in the rain,
As the music comes again.

I smile at couples rushing by,
With shared umbrellas held on high,
They are running from the rain,
As the music comes again.

I am just walking in the rain,
Where all the music sounds the same,
The rain feels good upon my face,
I really love this rainy place.

This showered avenue of rain,
Where all the music sounds the same,
Where all the songs go pitter-pat,
And there is nothing wrong with that.

I am just walking in the rain.

7.

DREAM GIRL.

She is a beauty of the sidewalk,
She turns so many heads around,
She knows that she is special,
As she just floats across the ground.

Dressed in Italian labels,
I guess a fragrance of Chanel,
Like a model on a catwalk,
My God, she wears it well.

I really, totally adore her,
From my office window chair,
As I watch her every evening,
I wish I was with her.

But I live in the real world,
A world of milk, not cream,
So, I know that she's beyond me,
But each evening I can dream.

8.

GIRL.

Your wild hair has never seen a brush,
Your tattooed arms are just wrong,
You talk like you've never cared enough,
Yet you still retain your charm.

Your vacant smile spoils a pretty face,
Your unkept nails are a mess,
Your jewellery is decades out of date,
And you haven't a clue how to dress.

But your eyes will light up most any room,
The way you move is sheer bliss,
You have a charisma which is unique,
And lips which beg to be kissed.

Your wild hair has never seen a brush,
Your tattooed arms are just wrong,
You talk like you've never cared enough,
Yet you still retain your charm.

9.

NOSTALGIA.

Some evenings I stroll down the dark cobbled lanes,
To the old part of town, far away from the norm,
Where past people walked and talked of their day,
In a time long since dead, in a world far away.

Through the shadows of time, I imagine this place,
Of how it once was in those dark long-lost days,
To the time of flat caps and bland hobnailed shoes,
A time of long dresses and black smoke-filled flues.

A pocket watch time, with horses not cars,
Street markets and bookshops, pianos in bars.
With pinches of snuff and pipe smoking gents,
Where ladies wore hats and small talk made sense.

As I breathe the nostalgia of this dark long-lost place,
I imagine myself drifting back through the years.
I can picture the sweeps and the young flower girls,
All dressed in rags, no silver or pearls.

The workhouse, the factory, the long-terraced street,
The gas lamps, the barrels, no shoes on young feet.
Although it seems distant, and much time has flown,
I still like to visit the places long gone.

10.

COMPLICATED.

You're complicated,
Don't debate it,
If you fake it,
You just make it,
Complicated.
Why say you love me,
For you also say to me,
You must be free,
So why do you still say,
That you love me.
You're complicated,
Don't debate it,
If you fake it,
You just make it,
Complicated.
Don't hold me tight,
Deep in the night,
Don't hold me tight,
Then want to fight,
Deep in the night.
You're complicated,
Don't debate it,
If you fake it,
You just make it
Complicated.
When your heart's sore,
You kiss me,
And you want to kiss me more
Then you hiss at me,
And walk right out the door.
You're complicated,
Oh... you're complicated.

11.

SUNDAY, SUNDAY.

Sunday, Sunday,
A day to rest my feet,
Slowly moving,
Through the quiet hours,
Sundays are so sweet,
And the gales don't blow,
On a peaceful day,
That moves so slow.

Sunday, Sunday,
If I had to dream,
Of the perfect day,
When my aches and pains,
Just fade away,
And I have the choice,
Of rest or play,
The day I'd choose,
Is, Sunday, Sunday.

Sunday, Sunday,
A day to rest my feet,
Slowly moving,
Through the quiet hours,
Sundays are so sweet,
Sunday, Sunday,
Sunday, Sunday,
Sunday, Sunday.

12.

LOST LOVE.

In the eyes of a girl sits a lonely heart,
Which hides from the light of the day,
Never knowing quite how to reveal itself,
As it shields from the stars faraway.

In her eyes there's a sadness which beauty hides,
From a world turning barren and blue,
As her heart breathes a sigh from a hope on high,
For a love which was honest and true.

So, she waits in the shadows and corridors,
Of a world which is sorry and dark.
She reflects on a love that has flown away,
And remembers the beat of its heart.

In the eyes of a girl sits a lonely heart,
Which hides from the light of the day,
Never knowing quite how to reveal itself,
As it shields from the stars faraway.

13.

WITH YOU I'LL STAND.

When you're lost and alone,
And life seems strange,
I'll take your hand.
When the world's at your throat,
And you feel afraid,
With you I'll stand.

Lose that frown, don't be down,
You know I'm here,
Each step of the way.
When it's dark or it's misty,
Or foggy babe,
I'll light your day.

When there's tears in your eyes,
Under darkened skies,
I'll kiss them dry.
When you're down on your knees,
And there's no way up,
I'll help you fly.

When you're lost and alone,
And life seems strange,
I'll take your hand.
When the world's at your throat,
And you feel afraid,
With you I'll stand.

14.

COFFEE TIME.

Every morning at eleven,
She walks past my table, at the same café,
And I feel like I'm in heaven,
Just knowing, she will pass my way.

A cup of coffee on my table,
A newspaper, that's just there for show,
I ain't wearing any label,
But I hope, she smiles my way once more.

Every morning at eleven,
She walks past my table, at the same café,
And I feel like I'm in heaven,
Just knowing, she will pass my way.

15.

ALONE.

You know I always loved you,
But I never could admit it, anyway.
And now you've gone and left me,
And I ain't got no other words to say.
So, I'm living in a world that I don't know,
Going to places I don't go,
Wearing a face gone melancholy too.
You're never there for me no more,
Searching for you don't break no law,
But you're breaking my heart,
The way that lovers do.

Tomorrow seems so distant,
Another restless night and broken dawn.
Yet, each morning I awaken,
Something deep inside me drives me on.
So, I'm living in a world that I don't know,
Going to places I don't go,
Wearing a face gone melancholy too.
You're never there for me no more,
Searching for you don't break no law,
But you're breaking my heart,
The way that lovers do,
Yes, you're breaking my heart,
The way that lovers do.

16.

THE GIRL WITH NO NAME.

As I sit on the beach,
I hope to see her,
The girl on the beach,
With the long golden hair.

I'm excited inside,
But my heart's feeling sore,
As the girl on the beach,
Walks past me once more.

Oh, my girl on the beach,
Why don't you notice me,
As I sit here alone,
For the whole world to see.

Oh, my girl on the beach,
My girl with no name,
You walk past me each day,
And each day's the same.

So, today I give up,
And just sit in the park,
I just stare at the ground,
Until it turns dark.

I hear a soft voice,
As words whisper my way,
'Where have you been,
I've been searching all day?'

As I lift my eyes,
She's standing right there,
My girl on the beach,
With the long golden hair.

17.

SITTING DOWN JOE.

Sitting down Joe,
With nowhere to go,
Glances at the clock.
While Jimmy Jack the lad,
In his rooftop pad,
Hears the band begin to rock.

Sitting down Joe,
With nowhere to go,
Will watch another TV show.
While Jimmy Jack the lad,
In his rooftop pad,
Is deciding on a place to go.

Sitting down Joe,
Begins to move slow,
To the kitchen for a cup of tea.
While Jimmy Jack the lad,
Leaves his rooftop pad,
Scouting all the clubs that be.

Sitting down Joe,
With nowhere to go,
Decides to try and read a book.
While Jimmy Jack the lad,
Ain't looking too sad,
As a woman throws him that look.

Sitting down Joe,
With nowhere to go,
Glances at the clock.
While Jimmy Jack the lad,
In his rooftop pad,
Hears the band begin to rock.

18.

I'M SORRY.

I can't hear the music for the evening rain,
But I can see the clouds up in the sky.
You never answer me when I call your name,
But I know you feel my pain as you walk by.

I'm sorry, I'm sorry, I never meant to hurt you,
I'm sorry, I'm sorry, I am.
Don't be this way, don't walk away,
I need to know that you will stay,
For you know I love you, all that I can.

If I smile at you, or blow a kiss,
The kiss may miss but I know you feel it,
But you don't smile at me, anymore.
If I touch your hand, you walk away,
And I'm left alone for another day,
With a heart which feels heavy, and sore.
I done a stupid thing and I don't know why,
I felt so bad when I made you cry,
You know it's true, I'll make it up to you.
Give me one more chance, I'm on my knees,
I know you can, for I know you love me,
Baby, I'm asking you, please.

I'm sorry, I'm sorry, I never meant to hurt you,
I'm sorry, I'm sorry, I am.
Don't be this way, don't walk away,
I need to know that you will stay,
For you know I love you, all that I can.

19.

EVENING SKY.

I'm standing gazing at the evening sky,
No need to say or give a reason why.
The starlight keeps on falling down on me,
The stars are shining for the world to see.

It mystifies and dances with my mind,
The more I look the more I seem to find.
The vastness of it all is what will be,
It helps us tell the tales of what we see.

As poets scan the skies for food,
They catch the words they always could.
So, even though all this is true,
Why is it so hard to say,
That I, love you.

20.

A WORLD IN FULL BLOOM.

Springtime, with the sun shining brightly,
And the songbirds all singing,
In a world of full bloom.
Winter, is only a memory now,
As springtime, sings in tune.

Walking, the path through a forest,
Where life feels so honest,
For the trees cannot lie.
Water, flows past daffodil crowds,
As a meadow, seems to sigh.

Your hand, resting in my hand,
With your smile, lighting the day.
Your eyes, reflecting the beauty I see,
As a cool breeze, drifts our way.

Springtime, with the sun shining brightly,
And the songbirds all singing,
In a world of full bloom.
Winter, is only a memory now,
As springtime, sings in tune.

SHE DANCE A LITTLE.

She talks so small,
But she stands so tall,
She moves like mist,
Beneath the glitter ball.
She's magic,
Oh, she's magic.

She moves so smooth,
Across the dancing floor,
Catching all the eyes,
As she dances more.
She's dancing,
Oh, she's dancing.

She wiggle wiggle hip a little,
Twist and turn,
The other girls watch,
As they crash and burn.
She's dancing,
Oh, she's dancing.

She glances,
As I catch her eye once more,
She drags me,
Onto the old dancefloor,
We're dancing,
And romancing.

I hold her close,
As the music slows,
She kiss a little sway a little,
As the music flows,
Within us,
While we're dancing.

22.

OLD MANS VOICE.

I’ve watched the ships sail down the river,
I’ve watched the mist roll down the Tyne,
I’ve walked the bridges and the banksides,
I’ve ate the fruit straight from the vine.

I never wanted much in my life,
Just to drift to simple things,
I didn’t dress up smart or look good,
I didn’t need no angels’ wings.

I remember all the old days,
Those day of graft, and sweat, and smiles,
The days when everything was normal,
Now seems a thousand distant miles.

Smiles in my heart shield saddened eyes,
I feel a lump form in my throat,
As more time passes now, I realise,
I feel so cold within my coat.

I’ve watched the ships sail down the river,
I’ve watched the mist roll down the Tyne,
I’ve walked the bridges and the banksides,
I’ve ate the fruit straight from the vine.

23.

ITALIAN BUTTERFLY.

At a street table at Café Tino,
Sipping at my cappuccino,
Watching sunlight's shadows,
Dance away.

Beautifully dressed Latin angels,
Walking past the café tables,
The Bella donnas always,
Pass this way.

Glancing at my magazine,
Seeing her in every dream,
Hoping she may pass my way,
Once more.

At a street table at Café Tino,
Sipping at my cappuccino,
Watching sunlight's shadows,
Dance away.

I sit here every day and night,
Watching butterflies in flight,
Praying that just one,
Will fly my way.

24.

SEPTEMBER CHANGING.

September changing brings the clouds,
The sun is on vacation,
With greyness all around.
The cutting winds are here once more,
They know that they're unwelcome,
But they've heard it all before.

Seasons are turning around again,
With sunshine lost to heavy rain.

My window acts as a warm shield,
Everything inside is cosy, light and clean,
Outside, the rain won't try to quit,
Painting patterns on my window,
With each and every single drip.

Summer has packed and flown away,
As Autumn shows her eyes today.

September changing brings the clouds,
The sun is on vacation,
With greyness all around.
The cutting winds are here once more,
They know that they're unwelcome,
But they've heard it all before.

And even though I hide away,
Peeping through my window,
Autumn shouts she's here to stay,
Once more.

25.

PETE AND SUE.

Never try to understand the ways of love,
Never even try to work it out,
Never try to understand the ways of love,
For you will never understand what love's about.

Peter fell in love across a crowded room,
It happened in a moment there and then,
And Susan hadn't even really noticed him,
Until he danced with her and then they danced again.

Gazing in her eyes he sensed a strange mystique,
Gazing in his eyes she sensed the same,
Holding her so close just felt so natural,
As they danced once more and then they danced again.

They felt like they had known each other all their lives,
So comfortable in each other's arms,
No spoken words were needed as they danced and danced,
Both hypnotized within each other's charms.

Never try to understand the ways of love,
Never even try to work it out,
Never try to understand the ways of love,
For you will never understand what love's about.

26.

CLUB CAVERNA.

I hear the music of the voices in the city,
As the flamenco dancer taps away the floor,
She is raw, she is sultry, she is pretty,
With dark eyes that you must follow more and more.

As she dances every step into your memory,
You will see her every time you close your eyes,
As she stares at you in visions cloaked in darkness,
Her cold charisma will leave you mesmerized.

Cigar smoke dances in the air of the Caverna,
The music dances to the center of your soul,
As the brown eyes of this wayward Ballerina,
Leave a vision far too vivid to control.

As you're drawn back to the night of the Caverna,
There's no importance of things which went before,
I am trapped deep inside the old Caverna,
As I'm haunted by the eyes I see once more.

27.

DANCING WITH RAINDROPS.

I love to walk out, on a rainy day,
I like to watch the raindrops, dance and play,
Can't you smell the scent, as the rain perfumes the trees,
Are you not pleased, that the rain came.

It paints a smile upon my face,
Each time I find a rainy place,
A place where I can splish, and splosh, and splash,
A place where I know my smiles will last,
And the rain, can't dampen how I feel,
It feels so real,
To share a dance, with raindrops.

28.

YOUR SMILE.

I don’t want to see you,
I don’t want to hold you,
I don’t want to kiss you.
I just want to look back,
At the way things were,
But not the way things are.

I remember how I saw you,
I remember how I held you,
I remember how I kissed you.
Distant memories dancing,
In my head romancing,
As I’m sitting at this bar.

We were both as one then,
And I simply can’t recall when,
We went our separate ways.
Minutes turned to hours then,
And I simply can’t recall when,
The hours turned to days.

No, I don’t want to see you,
I don’t want to hold you,
I don’t want to kiss you.
I just want to sit here,
Slowly drinking cold beer,
And remembering those days.

29.

MIDNIGHT'S STREET.

When I'm lonely, I walk,
The long midnight street.
Without you by my side,
My life's incomplete.

As memories drift,
Across cloudy skies,
The rain pouring down,
Hides the stars from my eyes.

A cold wind cuts through,
And I fight with the rain,
As pictures of you,
Come to me, once again.

Each night I pray,
That, once more we will meet,
Until that day,
I must walk midnight's street.

30.

WHY.

In the wind and in the rain,
I walk and search for you again.
I still hear your voice, with ears ringing,
I still taste your lips, with heart singing,
But when I reach out, for your touch,
Reflections never, seem enough,
But I still hope, to find you.

As my days turn into night,
You're hiding somewhere out of sight.
Yet my heart, just can't give up on you,
I won't believe, that our love's not true,
And I wonder, night and day,
What made you up, and walk away,
I just can't live, without you.

On the night you said goodbye,
I watched each star fall from the sky.
I'm left with memories, of how things were,
I talk to you, but you're not there,
As my memories, drive me each, single step,
I can't accept,
That you're not here, beside me.

So, in the wind and in the rain,
I walk and search for you again.
I still hear your voice, with ears ringing,
I still taste your lips, with heart singing,
But when I reach out, for your touch,
Reflections never, seem enough,
But I still hope, to find you.

31.

THROUGH MIDNIGHT.

Climbing out of a lonely bed,
Thinking of the things she said,
Looking at the way things are,
As I get dressed to drive my car,
Through midnight.

Driving down a city street,
Driving to where lovers meet,
Turning on my radio,
Slow slow quick and quick quick slow,
Through midnight.

Rolling to that special place,
The place I most recall her face,
A moonlit walk, a kiss from her,
Her stunning eyes, her auburn hair,
Through midnight.

My midnight lady is gone for good,
She moved away, as she said she would,
I get a message as I stand alone,
A goodbye text on my telephone,
Through midnight.

32.

WRITING ON WATER.

I just wanted to tell you,
About how I feel today,
So, I picked a pen up,
In that good old-fashioned way.

I've been staring at paper,
But the pen won't make its mark,
I've been writing on water,
As the words just drift apart.

How do I write down,
The way you move, the way you look,
How do I write down,
That my heart's an open book.

I watched you dance once,
On one far off summer night,
You moved with charisma,
From shadows into light.

That night I first saw you,
My body felt the heat,
That night I first saw you,
My heart just skipped a beat.

And since that first evening,
I dream each day of you,
You don't even know me,
So, I don't know what to do.

(continued)

How do I write down,
The way you move, the way you look,
How do I write down,
That my heart's an open book.

I just wanted to tell you,
About how I feel today,
So, I picked a pen up,
In that good old-fashioned way.

I've been staring at paper,
But the pen won't make its mark,
I've been writing on water,
As the words just drift apart.

33.

WHEN YOU RETURN.

Starlight and moonbeams,
Reflect from your eyes,
White doves and rainbows,
Fly in the skies.
Christmas trees and mistletoe,
Early morning dew,
Many things come back to me,
When I am with you.

When I'm alone,
Darkness falls,
Winds blow wild and cold.
The streets I walk,
Are haunted streets,
When I'm all, alone.

But, when you, come back to me,
My world is fresh and new,
Nothing then, can frighten me,
When I am, with you.

No haunted streets,
Where darkness calls,
Just early morning dew.
The flowers return,
The sky is bright,
When I'm back with you.

34.

FAREWELL.

Shaking loose the strings of my heart,
Whenever we part,
How I miss you.
Spinning in the vaults of my mind,
As I leave you behind,
So, I kiss you.

Now I'm leaving and I don't know where,
I'll only know it, once I'm there,
The one thing that is true,
Will be you.
Yeah, I'm leaving and I don't know where,
I'll only know it, once I'm there,
But one thing that is true,
Will be you.

Shaking loose the strings of my heart,
Whenever we part,
How I miss you.
Spinning in the vaults of my mind,
As I leave you behind,
So, I kiss you.

Don't look for me, when I'm not here,
Don't worry and don't shed a tear,
Just close your pretty eyes,
And I'll kiss you.

35.

BROKEN MIRROR.

I saw her walking on a lonely, rainy, city street,
The way she moved,
The way she looked,
Just, the way of her,
A portrait of sheer elegance.

Then I discovered who she was,
A superstar,
A star of stars,
A headliner, known afar,
Who would never know, she stole my heart.
With her,
An ordinary guy like me,
Would be,
Without a chance,
Of any romance.

I saw him standing on a lonely, rainy, city street,
His relaxed stance,
The way he smiled,
The way he looked,
Was strong and true.

He could never know, he stole my heart,
I never did know, who he was.
Yet, I think of him most every day,
The stranger, who took my breath away,
I pray one day he'll smile my way,
And,
Just,
Maybe say,
Hello.

36.

BLACK AND WHITE STREETS.

Black and white streets,
Black and white skies,
Seeing these streets,
Through back and white eyes.

You couldn't know it,
You'd never get near,
You couldn't feel it,
Unless you're from here,
These black and white streets.

It's easy to explain,
What this place means to me,
A place full of memories,
All plain to see,
On these black and white streets.

Memories of childhood,
Blasts from the past,
Memories of loved ones,
The memories last,
On these black and white streets.

We children of Tyneside,
Feel all that we should,
For deep down inside us,
Flows black and white blood,
From the black and white streets.

(continued)

Black and white streets,
Black and white skies,
Seeing these streets,
Through black and white eyes.

You couldn’t know it,
You’d never get near,
You couldn’t feel it,
Unless you’re from here,
These back and white streets.

ORDINARY JOE.

I never thought,
I'd ever see a girl like you,
A girl that looks the way you do,
A girl like you.

I was just an ordinary Joe,
Going where Joes go,
On an ordinary night,
Until my heart took flight.

You smiled at me from a window high,
That's all it took,
You changed my world,
With just one look.

Some evenings, I will walk your street,
In the hope to catch your smile once more,
Be it rain or stars, cold or warm,
I still glance up to the third floor.

A single glance is all I pray,
As each short moment passes by,
In the hope that you may glance my way,
One day, as I glance up on high.

(Continued)

I have rehearsed a blowing kiss,
Should you notice me once more,
I hope it will not seem too bold,
Should you smile from the third floor.

I'm just an ordinary Joe,
Going where Joes go,
Simply hoping, while strolling time,
To see once more your golden smile.

Maybe you'll never look at me,
And maybe you won't want to know,
Or even care at what you see,
After all,
I'm just an ordinary Joe.

38.

ANGELINA.

Angelina, Angelina,
Hear me calling,
Even though I know that you're so far away.
Oh, my darling Angelina,
I am falling,
Through a dream which seems so real most every day.

As I gaze up to the heavens, Angelina,
I can see your sweet face smiling from the stars.

And as I walk alone,
Neath the evening moon,
I just close my eyes,
Neath the moonlit skies,
And I can feel your heart beating, Angelina,
From this dark and lonely place,
I call my home.

39.

RAIN IN MY HEART.

Even though, my eyes have stopped smiling,
Even though, the sun does not shine,
Don't think, I'm just the fool on the hill,
Just because, sadness now fills my eyes.

Even though, my heart is not singing,
Even though, my lips miss your touch,
Don't think, I'm feeling lonesome for you,
Even though, I miss you so much.

Each evening, as my tears soak my pillow,
Each evening, as the sky seems so vast,
I gaze up, and watch as our love fades away,
And tomorrow, gets lost in the past.

But don't think, that my heart has stopped beating,
And don't think, that dry lips cannot kiss,
For I know, I can be as strong as before,
I can be, as I was, just once more.

So, even though, my eyes have stopped smiling,
Even though, the sun does not shine,
Don't dare think, I am the fool on the hill,
Because sadness, now fills my eyes.

40.

OLD ROBERT.

I will remember, old Robert,
As, he walked down the street,
Gathering half cigarettes,
From under his feet.

He walked and he wandered,
With no place called home,
No talk of his past,
Or, where he came from.

He never complained,
His face full of smiles,
In his old, tattered raincoat,
He'd wander for miles.

The days were so cold,
With wind, snow, and ice,
The place Robert sheltered,
Wasn't so nice.

They found him one morning,
In an old, ruined place,
No windows or doors,
Just that smile on his face.

He walked and he wandered,
With no place called home,
No talk of his past,
Or, where he came from.

41.

BLUE SKIES.

Why do all the clouds drain out on me,
When the skies are blue for all the other guys,
Why do sad thoughts still follow me,
When I want to be just like the other guys.

Things are always changing,
And I really don't know why,
They say the sun is shining,
When all I see is a darkened sky.

Why do all the clouds drain out on me,
When the skies are blue for all the other guys,
Why do sad thoughts still follow me,
When I just want to be like the other guys.

As the streets crumble below me,
I hear them crash and burn as I walk by,
I look into a mirror,
But all I see is a soaked through guy.

Why do all the clouds drain out on me,
When the skies are blue for all the other guys,
Why do sad thoughts still follow me,
When I want to be just like the other guys.

42.

THE ROAD TO DON'T KNOW WHERE.

You'll find your past,
In photographs,
And memories you share.
Old music sings,
Of special things,
And when you were there.
But you'll never know,
Where you're sure to go,
And what that road may tell.
For the future hides away,
So well.

The words on a page,
Tell of their age,
When they speak to you.
Yet ancient words,
Can seem absurd,
And don't read so true.
But you'll never know,
Where you're sure to go,
And what that road may tell.
For the future hides away,
So well.

Loves of the past,
Remain and last,
In memories of things dear.
And they will always sing to you,
And make you shed a tear.
But you'll never know,
Where you're sure to go,
And what that road may tell.
For the future hides away, So well.

43.

ROSE IN THE SNOW.

On a winter's night, in a frozen street,
Crowds walk on icy ground.
Neath the neon lights, over trampled dreams,
A silent glance is found.

For midst the crowd sits an angel's face,
A moment froze in time.
Below the snows, neath the neon lights,
Our eyes embrace and smile.

I moved towards from whence she glanced,
To where she still should be.
But standing there amidst the crowds,
Her eyes are lost to me.

Through crowded streets I walked alone,
Still searching her embrace.
With saddened eyes, I searched once more,
She'd gone and left no trace.

Each snowy night on frosted streets,
I walk on icy ground.
Over trampled dreams, I seek that smile,
Or vision I once found.

I search each city street,
I search each barren field.
I search each face, each smile,
I search my dream revealed.

(continued)

Each day I live the same routine,
Walking snows in winter chill.
Each day I think she's lost for good,
And yet I seek her still.

In barren fields I walk alone,
Brittle ice snaps under toe.
All seems lost but for one thing,
A single rose stands in the snow.

44.

WALKING WITH THE CLOUDS.

I was talking to the trees,
And whistling with the breeze,
While showering with the rain.
I watched some falling leaves drift by,
As a rainbow split a darkened sky,
And the forest called my name.

The clouds were floating past me,
As a scarecrow stooped to ask me,
'Can you please tell me the time?'
As I got busy speaking,
The words that I was seeking,
Slowly melted to a mime.

With small creatures watching closely,
And a waterfall that mostly,
Threw mist into the air.
I lay down and I relaxed,
On a bank of dampened grass,
With the wind still in my hair.

I was talking to the trees,
And whistling with the breeze,
While showering with the rain.
I watched some falling leaves drift by,
As a rainbow split a darkened sky,
And the forest called my name.

45.

LETTING GO.

She could see I loved her,
Even when I walked away,
Smiling briefly at each other,
No other words to say.
Both of us could fight no more,
We never stood a chance,
The writing had been on the wall,
To end our long romance.

I see her smile in every face,
Her words in every voice.
We tried so hard to work it out,
But we never had a choice.
I wear the scarf she used to wear,
To feel she's close to me,
It still carries the perfume,
Of how things used to be.

The streets I walk seem longer,
And the moonlight doesn't last,
The flowers are all wilting,
As an old man shuffles past.
Some children with their laughter,
Helped me try to force a smile,
Then the sky just clouded over,
As I sat, the longest time.

(continued)

I wonder how she’s doing,
Whose hand is in her hand,
The calendar says three months past,
Like grains of timeless sand.
Soon the autumn leaves will fall,
Bringing chilling winds and more,
And I will have to stand alone,
Like a stranger on a shore.

REGRETS.

I was born on the backstreets of Tyneside,
In the days of hard times and hard work,
Where nothing was taken for granted,
But I don't remember much pain or much hurt.

The holes in my shoes let in water,
The knees of my jeans were not there,
In our house each winter we shivered,
But that was normal, so we didn't care.

In my twenties I started a business,
I remembered each lesson I'd learnt,
I'd met all the conmen and tricksters,
I was cool, so I'd never get burnt.

In my thirties I wore a gold Rolex,
My car was a silver Rolls Royce,
In the summer I lazed in the tropics,
In the winter I had little choice,
St Moritz.

I still think of the backstreets of Tyneside,
With a massive daft smile on my face,
For as I look at the wealth which surrounds me,
I often feel well out of place.

(continued)

I dream of the backstreets of Tyneside,
And yearn for the place of my youth,
I wish I was back there this moment,
I miss it so much, that's the truth.

I walked away from the backstreets of Tyneside,
With a mission, a plan, and a cause,
But if I could just turn the clock back,
I would return to just how it was,
Yes, I would.

47.

HOMECOMING.

I’ve been away from home far too long,
I’ve seen what I needed to see.
I’ve touched the hot sun and the chilled winter wind,
Yet my roots always stayed true to me.

In deserts afar, or forests on high,
I could still feel the beat of my home.
Just calling me in from some far distant land,
Reminding me where I came from.

I’m so close that I can almost taste,
The history, the warmth, and the Tyne.
The street talk, the friendship, the trust and the soul,
Of a people who’ll always be mine.

As I walk along the quayside,
Then the bridge with its lights burning bright,
A tear hits my eye for the first time in years,
For I know that I’ve reached home tonight.

I’ve been away from home far too long,
I’ve seen what I needed to see.
I’ve touched the hot sun and the chilled winter wind,
Yet my roots always stayed true to me.

48.

CHILLED ROMANCE.

Hold my hand and let me guide you,
Through the winter's icy snows,
I'll place my coat across your shoulders,
Each time a cold wind blows.

With me right here beside you,
Let me see your carefree smile,
Let me gaze into your eyes girl,
As we walk that extra mile.

I know your parents don't approve girl,
I'm from the wrong side of the tracks,
But don't dismiss me out of sight girl,
A little time is all I ask.

So, hold my hand and let me guide you,
Through the winter's icy snows,
I'll place my coat across your shoulders,
Each time a cold wind blows.

49.

FOREST OF LOVE.

Looking at the trees around the lake,
Picturing the changes and the reason,
Gentle waters ripple with the rain,
Golden fallen leaves reflect the season.

The darkened skies throw anger to the wind,
A blustery song is wild and set to shiver,
Within the trees a barren forest rests,
Amid the screaming torrent of a river.

The sleeping forest rests until the spring,
She dreams through all the cold of days which follow,
She bows her head and slowly rests her eyes,
And patiently awaits the long tomorrow.

But her beauty is not lost in these cold times,
Dressed golden brown with subtle shades of amber,
As the pearls of rain which hang around her neck,
Catch rays of light that glisten and meander.

All through the barren months she stands with pride,
With swaying movement, colour, and charisma,
And even when she's feeling cold inside,
The beauty flows around her like a river.

(continued)

So, I smile and blow a kiss upon the wind,
To wish her luck and pledge my love forever,
As I turn away, I take one final glance,
Then walk away to leave her at her leisure.

Remembering the trees around the lake,
Picturing the changes and the reason,
Gentle waters ripple with the rain,
Golden fallen leaves reflect the season.

50.

END OF SHOW.

You did not know,
One day you'd find that I would leave you,
But you did not care,
Quite enough to make me stay.

I won't be back,
Because I never felt you loved me,
So, leave me be,
Stop phoning me, each night and day.

All I hear,
Is that you're sorry, or you miss me,
Or you say,
That you'll change and treat me good.

In seven years,
You never once said that you love me,
In seven years,
You never once showed that you could.

So, now I'm gone,
And I feel free, and I feel happy,
So, stop the calls,
Don't contact me, just let me go.

You had your chance,
A thousand times, but did not take it,
The play is done,
The curtain's down,
I've left the show.

51.

I DON'T NEED MUSIC.

I don't need music,
To serenade.
The words I think, the words I like, are all I need.

Can't you hear me,
As I write.
My heart is calling out to you, tonight.

I can touch you,
When I'm not there.
Can't you feel my blowing kiss in the night air.

I can reach you,
You know it's true.
For you smile back over the miles, when I feel blue.

I don't need music,
To serenade.
I know you hear my silent thoughts, as they cascade.

So, close your eyes now,
Your dreams are bright.
I'll serenade you without music through the night.

52.

SUNNY DAYS.

I can't hear the rain, lashing my window,
Even though I know it's pouring down.
I only see the sun, every morning,
Since the day that you came back to town.

As I walk in the rain, it cannot touch me,
It just misses and falls on either side.
With a smile back on my face, I feel happy,
Knowing you are right here by my side.

I just glance at you, when we're out walking,
As your clear blue eyes, light up my way.
I adore your voice, when we are talking,
On yet another bright sunny day.

I can't hear the rain, lashing my window,
Even though I know it's pouring down.
I only see the sun. every morning,
Since the day that you came back to town.

53.

SUNDAY MORNING BLUES.

Sunday morning feeling down,
As I walk an empty street,
There is no one left around,
And no one I want to meet.

I saw you kiss him late last night,
That way you looked into his eyes,
I did not know so could not fight,
You were feeding me on lies.

Why did I not see through you,
How did you hide it every day.
What I know I saw is true,
How did you hide it all away.

As I walk this empty street,
I understand that I was blind,
I put all my trust in you,
Now I must leave it all behind.

Sunday morning feeling blue,
As I walk an empty street,
There is no one left around,
And no one I want to meet.

54.

LONESOME COWBOY.

It's three in the morning, and I sit here yawning,
Flushing my night's rest away.
You ain't come home yet, and my mind is dead set,
Once more you've decided to stray.

You know that I love you, and my love is so true,
I won't say a word once you're home.
But darling I'm missing, the lips that he's kissing,
Since they decided to roam.

You don't know that I know, the places that you go,
And whose hand you're holding each time.
As I sit here drinking, my sore head's done thinking,
Not knowing if you are still mine.

It's three in the morning, and I sit here yawning,
Flushing my night's rest away.
You ain't come home yet, and my mind is dead set,
Once more you've decided to stray.

CHILDHOOD MEMORIES OF MY HOMETOWN.

The ferries on the river,
With cranes along the way.
Cardboard in my play-shoes,
Another rainy day.

Coal trucks near the Cokie's,
Blackberry bushes either side,
Toughened little street kids,
With our eyes all opened wide.

Hiding under the table,
As the rent man taps the door,
To pretend our house is empty,
But I think he knew the score.

Chips from Finchale fish shop,
With extra batter please,
Washed down with juice or pop,
And serves with mushy peas.

The forty-seven bus,
That took you to the town.
Everyone dressed up,
We could hardly have dressed down.

Or a day at South Shields beach,
A towel as a seat,
Then building castles in the sand,
That really was a treat.

(continued)

In the summer, our weekends,
Were football in the park,
We'd leave just after breakfast,
And return before it's dark.

Tyneside in the sixties,
Not frilled, not gold, not pearled,
Just the way it used to be,
I wouldn't change it for the world.

56.

THE GEORDIE MOON.

The Geordie moon has many colours,
The River Tyne takes many turns,
Old ferryboats are gone forever,
But every night the moon returns.

The ships we built are distant memories,
Yet in men's eyes still shines the pride.
And though the ships sank like the ferries,
I still miss them, deep inside.

I miss the noises of the shipyards,
I miss friends faces, long since gone.
Maybe, I'm living in the past now,
But please don't say that, that is wrong.

The Geordie moon has many colours,
The River Tyne's still shining bright.
Maybe, I dream like many others,
I still chase rainbows in the night.

57.

STREETS OF DREAMS.

I walk old lanes where I once played,
On the cobblestones where friends were made.
Girls with pigtails, skipping rope,
In the days of less, and hard to cope,
On these streets, of dreams and hope.

Down these streets of many names,
Children played their daily games.
In this place, where no one now goes,
I still picture the boys in their ragged clothes,
On these streets of highs and lows.

We all moved on and turned a page,
From this far off, distant, long-lost age,
But from this old nostalgic scene,
All the images to me, are real,
As are the memories I live and feel.

I feel these streets live on, and be,
For in myself I plainly see,
These streets are such a part of me.
Their whispered laughter sounds so fine,
Bright distant echoes, of a long lost in time.

58.

AN UNEXPECTED CHRISTMAS GIFT.

I cleared my eyes when I first saw you,
I never asked where you came from,
I only know I really missed you,
And now you're back where you belong.

Those lonely nights are far behind me,
Your loving arms are here once more,
You just sailed off one starlit evening,
But now you've drifted back to shore.

I cleared my eyes when I first saw you,
I never asked where you came from,
I only know I really missed you,
And now you're back where you belong.

59.

SPIDER.

She’s playing in the game,
She’s playing in the game of life.
Nothing’s quite the same,
Now she’s learnt to roll the dice.

A swivel of the hips,
Painted eyes that light a room.
Rouge upon her lips,
Taunting guys to follow soon.

She spins her chosen web,
The shining threads capture the light.
A man gets trapped inside,
She takes him down into the night.

Then she strikes at speed,
Her prey would never stand a chance.
All she needed to succeed,
Was that first and sultry glance.

She’s playing in a game,
She’s playing in the game of life.
Nothing’s quite the same,
Now she’s learnt to roll the dice.

THE SIXTIES.

Mobiles were called walkie-talkies,
A computer was known as your brain,
Text messages were secret notes,
And celebs had a skill in the main.

Sat-navs were unfolded road maps,
Which believe it or not, got you there,
Talking sats, were back seat drivers,
Who gave you a pain in the ear.

Everyone still had a twin-tub,
My gran had a mangle as well,
Wooden floorboards meant you were poor,
With carpets as expensive as hell.

A bath meant waiting your turn,
A shower was a dance in the rain,
The kids got a scrub in the sink,
It polished them up all the same.

Credit was bought on the provi,
A man knocked your door for the rent,
A lot of meals came from the chip shop,
With holiday the new word for tent.

Tudor crisps were still number one,
Spangles old English were good,
Corrie appeared on the T.V.
And instant mash murdered the spud.

(continued)

Awesome was probably awesome,
A sweet pastry was known as a tart,
Wicked was somebody nasty,
A selfie, a common wet fart.

There is nothing wrong with nostalgia,
As memories mould who we are,
So, take a look back in time now and then,
And remember that clapped out first car.

61.

THROUGH THE LOOKING GLASS.

You changed your world of have and hold,
And traded it for streets of gold.
You’re living out a fairytale,
And drifting where few others sail.

The terraced streets you have declined,
With faithful friends all left behind,
The streets on which you used to walk,
Old friends of which you never talk.

I don’t know what your mirror shows,
Or how deep a reflection goes,
I’m sure it only sees a shell,
For it cannot look inside as well.

It will not see the girl I knew,
Her smiling face with eyes of blue,
The girl where every day was fine,
That special girl who once was mine.

You changed your world of have and hold,
And traded it for streets of gold.
You’re living out a fairytale,
And drifting where few others sail.

LONESOME GAMBLER BLUES.

Teardrops falling in my coffee,
Two sugars or a spoonful of honey,
No money in my pockets today,
I gotta learn to walk away.

Drew two aces from a split pack,
Went in heavy trying to win my own cash back,
The dealer turned two threes and a two,
Which gave a winning hand to you.

I will never ever endeavour,
To understand why I lose,
I can only feel the cash slowly,
Draining out of my shoes.

Light swinging in a dark room,
Stained walls around a table of green baize,
Straight faces that I'm trying to read,
Not knowing when to fold or lead.

Smoke filling up the dark room,
Lost it all so I guess I'll go home soon,
Not knowing how to pay the next bill,
I never did and never will.

I will never ever endeavour,
To understand why I lose,
I can only feel the cash slowly,
Draining out through my shoes.

(continued)

Teardrops falling in my coffee,
Two sugars or a spoonful of honey,
No money in my pockets today,
I gotta learn to walk away.

63.

DAFFODILS.

Wooden chalets, on a hillside,
Framed by springtime's host of daffodils,
In a valley, near a mountain,
In a country, far away.
Little children, chase each other,
On a hillside framed in daffodils,
And the children, with their laughter,
Can be heard throughout the day.

And the sunlight, casts its shadows,
Over fields all full of daffodils,
And the sunlight, holds a rainbow,
Which encircles fields of gold.
For the pictures, that are painted,
Reflect a beauty for the world to see,
Subtle colours, gentle colours,
Behaving as they're never told.

And this hillside, full of daffodils,
Full of perfume, full of many things,
Makes your eyes weep, makes your lips smile,
Makes you feel like you have wings.
So, you dream of wooden chalets,
As you sleep on a bed of daffodils,
And you lie there, till the sun sets,
And the stars bring evening's chills.

64.

DON'T GO.

Don't go throwing, all your love dear,
Spread and trampled on the floor.
Pick it up, and hold it close dear,
Just like the way things were before.

Don't accuse me, of being unfaithful,
Don't listen to, an evil lie.
Don't you know dear, that I love you,
And there's no need for you to cry.

I've done some good things, and some bad things,
But no bad things done to you.
Please don't listen, to what they're saying,
I swear my love to you is true.

So, don't go throwing, all your love dear,
Spread and trampled on the floor.
Pick it up, and hold it close dear,
Just like the way things were before.

65.

DONNA.

My Donna, my sweet Donna, are you perfect,
Are you all the things I really think you are,
You blossom in the springtime, my sweet Donna,
As the world admires your beauty from afar.

As you elegantly dance away the hours,
Is it true that you're an angel in disguise.
As I watch you orchestrate the April showers,
Could it be I see our future in your eyes.

Oh, sweet Donna, please, speak the words I need,
When I'm close to you, when our hearts are true.
And feel the moment, my sweet donna,
Just as a blossom tastes the kiss of morning dew.

Let me hold you and caress you, my sweet Donna,
With our hearts entwined we'll feel as we are one.
Let me even see you notice me, sweet Donna,
Or if all my hopes of loving you, are gone.

Sweet Donna, please, speak the words I need,
When I am close to you, as my heart feels blue.
Let me know if you can love me, my sweet Donna,
For all my lonely dreams, could then come true.

My Donna, my sweet Donna, are you perfect,
Are you all the things I really think you are.
You blossom in the springtime, my sweet Donna,
As the world admires your beauty, from afar.
Oh, sweet Donna.

THEY NEVER PHONE.

Will anybody love me,
Will anybody care,
Will anybody look at,
A thirty something awkward girl,
Is anybody there.

I get nervous when I speak,
The words all come out wrong,
The more I talk the worse it gets,
And by then I've talked too long.

Will anybody love me,
Will anybody care,
Can anyone see past my mask,
To the person inside there.

I've never learnt to listen,
My dress sense makes men stare,
I try to squeeze into tight clothes,
Which I know I shouldn't wear.

Will anybody love me,
Will anybody care,
Will anybody try to see,
The person who is there.

I know that I'm not graceful,
Or elegant at all,
When I try to be a lady,
Each time I'm sure to fall.

(continued)

Will anybody love me,
Will anybody care,
Will anybody look at,
A thirty something awkward girl,
Is anybody there.

67.

JEZEBEL.

Don't you know girl,
Breaking hearts girl,
Ain't the nicest thing to do.
I know your history,
It trampled on me,
So, I know these words are true.

I met your new guy,
Who's now your old guy,
He was sitting, feeling blue.
How many hearts girl,
Must you break girl,
Before you see it's down to you.

Oh, don't you know girl,
Breaking hearts girl,
Ain't the nicest thing to do.
I know your history,
It trampled on me,
So, I know these words are true.

68.

ONCE MORE.

I walk silent streets alone,
The music is all sleeping,
Though memories hang on,
My broken heart is weeping.

Does she kiss the way I do,
Does she hold you just as tight,
Will she whisper words of love,
As you journey through the night.

Does she watch you as you sleep,
Does she smile each time you sigh,
Will she nurse you if you're sick,
Will she do the same as I.

In the shadows of the night,
Do you ever think of me,
Do you ever hold a light,
For how things used to be.

From the beating of my heart,
And with every breath I breathe,
With every step I take,
I can't really believe.

Each evening is the same,
My heart has lost its home,
Unanswered questions haunt me,
As I wander streets alone,
Once more.

69.

LIVING THE DREAM.

Like the stars across the sky,
Or the waves that cross the sea,
Like the mountains standing high,
Or the leaves upon a tree.

Like the ripples on a lake,
Or a waterfall at dawn,
Like the beating of my heart,
Showing where my dreams come from.

All the things that I can see,
Show the way that life can be.

Like a forest's autumn leaves,
Or the perfume of the spring,
Like a meadow in full bloom,
Or a snowy winter chill.

Like warm sand below my feet,
Or the early morning dew,
And the way you set me free,
When you made my dreams come true.

These are the things that I can see,
Every moment you're with me.

70.

STORMY DAYS.

Sitting in the wings of a storm,
In a corner of calm, missing your face.
Watching as the dark clouds drift by,
With no sun in the sky, there is no trace.

Why we argued, I still don't know,
Now I'm walking with no place to go.
My life feels very dark,
Since we've been apart.

Hoping for a glimpse of the sun,
But I'm still on the run, from a past life.
I still recall your face every day,
But you're so far away, in a new life.

I keep going, but I don't know where,
All I'm knowing, is you won't be there.
No where to call my home,
I'm so alone.

Sitting in the wings of a storm,
In a corner of calm, missing your face.
Watching as the dark clouds drift by,
With no sun in the sky, there is no trace.

I keep going, but I don't know where,
All I'm knowing. is you won't be there.
No where to call my home,
I'm so alone.

THE STOTTIE CAKE EXPRESS.

Some pease pudding,
From the butcher,
That you slap on a slab of stottie cake,
Then you add on,
A slice of boiled ham,
And that's your bait,
For another day.
So, you wrap it,
Up in paper,
And stick it inside your haversack,
Then you walk down,
To the ferry,
To cross the Tyne,
And make some pay.

And you go home,
And your son says,
He'd climb a mountain for a bag of Tudor crisps,
And your wife says,
That your tea's done,
So, you eat,
Your beans on toast.
And you sit down,
And watch the T.V.
Coz it's Corrie and then The Likely Lads,
So, you drink your cup of hot tea,
Then you dream,
Of the Sunday roast.

(continued)

On the weekend,
It's the legion,
Where you drink brown ale from a half pint glass,
As your wife,
Is playing bingo,
So, there's a chance you can pay a bill.
And the rent man,
And the milk man,
And the coal man and the provi man,
Knock your door,
To get their money,
When they know you're never in.

Some pease pudding,
From the butcher,
That you slap on a slab of stottie cake,
And then you add on,
A slice of boiled ham,
And that's your bait,
For another day.
So, you wrap it,
Up in paper,
And stick it inside your haversack,
Then you walk down,
To the ferry,
To cross the Tyne,
And make some pay.

72.

GEORDIE SHORE.

As I walk along the Geordie shore,
It looks the way it always looked before.
But my mother tells me much has changed,
And how her life's been rearranged,
And how things never seem the same no more.

How her friends all used to visit her,
To sit and gossip long days way.
How everyone was closer then,
A family of us and them,
Times lost, and just a memory today.

I could see the sadness in her eyes,
And all at once I realized,
This lovely woman's world had changed a lot.
Her words were coming from the past,
Understanding things don't last,
Remembering the times that time forgot.

As I walk along the Geordie shore,
It looks the way it always looked before.
But my mother tells me much has changed,
And how her life's been rearranged,
And how things never seem the same no more.

KISS ME QUICK AND CANDYFLOSS.

Remember the old coach trips,
When half the street would go.
Although most of us had nowt,
We'd still get our day out.

Sometimes there'd be a few trip buses,
Travelling nose to tail.
We picked a date, then took a chance,
And prayed it wouldn't rain.

Women all wore beehives,
Guys all wore a quiff.
Mam had took her curlers out,
And dad smoked his wills wiffs.

The radio played Beatle songs,
Backed up by all our singalongs.
Sandwiches and flasks of tea,
Unscheduled stops to take a pee.

A café stop along the way,
To stretch our legs, my mam would say.
Anticipation, mile on mile,
Even granda forced a smile.

And then onto the seaside,
With fish and chips and beer.
Kids got candy-floss and donkey rides,
Then slots along the pier.

(continued)

With granny playing bingo,
As mam bathes in the sun.
The boys chat up bikini girls,
Until the day is done.

Then back onto the coach,
With loads to talk about.
You know, it must be nearly fifty years,
Since our street had a day out.

74.

THE GAME OF LIFE.

The game of life is very strange,
You play your cards, but it won't change,
No matter what hand's dealt to you,
You play it out till the game is through.
And life will take no prisoners,
And life will have no friend,
And all you win are memories,
In the end.

If you're dealt twos or faces,
Life holds all the aces,
So, no matter what you choose,
In the end you'll lose.
For life will take no prisoners,
And life will have no friend,
And all you win are memories,
In the end.

As life plays out with a stacked deck,
The crooked game is all you get,
And then right at the end of play,
All your cards are blown away.
For life will take no prisoners,
And life will have no friend,
And all you win are memories,
In the end.

75.

L'AMOUR.

Love,
Or as the French would say,
Call it L'amour.
Oh, how I love her more and more,
As each moment passes,
I love her.

Embrace,
Or as the French would say,
Embrasser.
Oh, how I love to hold her tight,
Each time we're together,
I love her.

Blue eyes,
Or as the French would say,
Les yeux bleus.
Her eyes shine like the stars,
That's maybe because,
I love her.

Her smile,
Or as the French would say,
Son sourire.
Oh, how her smile lights up my day,
In every way,
I love her.

Her beauty,
Or as the French would say,
Sa beaute.
Shines like a thousand dancing lights,
Of romantic nights,
And I love her.

76.

GIRL ON A BEACH.

Sunny Sunday, lazy Sunday,
Spent singing out a song.
Children's laughter, echoes past her,
As she daydreams all alone.

Sunny Sunday, lazy Sunday,
Chase the ripples from the sea.
Golden waters gently glisten,
Reflecting light to thee.

Sunny Sunday, lazy Sunday,
With the aroma of the spring.
She's relaxing, softly basking,
Heat waves hovering.

Sunny Sunday, lazy Sunday,
She slowly rests her eyes.
Sunny Sunday, lazy Sunday,
A Sunday consciousness denies.

77.

FIRST DATE THOUGHTS.

Meet me at the railway clock at nine,
Please don't make excuses,
Say that you'll be mine,
Meet me at the railway clock at nine.

Last night when she said we should meet again,
My head just started spinning,
A shock wave ran through me,
Meet me at the railway clock at nine.

I'm getting ready now to go to him,
I'm praying that he'll be there,
To miss would be a sin,
Meet me at the railway clock at nine.

I'm nervous like I've never been before,
I'm floating off the ground,
And I cannot make a sound,
Meet me at the railway clock at nine.

Meet me at the railway clock at nine,
Please don't make excuses,
Say that you'll be mine,
Meet me at the railway clock at nine.

YOU LEFT ME BABE.

I know you left me babe,
For screwing up that one last time,
Oh, you left me babe,
Even though our hearts entwine,
Yes, you left me babe,
I know you left me babe.

When I walk at night,
I still believe that you are near,
And when they talk to me,
It's only your voice that I hear,
Or when the stars shine bright,
In each eye there sits a tear,
Because you left me babe.

If the wind blows,
I hear it call your name,
And if it doesn't,
I hear it just the same,
And the people,
Say it's such a shame,
That you left me babe.

I tried to phone you,
But you wouldn't take my call.
I wrote a letter,
Then simply pinned it to the wall,
Just to remind me,
That I know you'll never call,
Because you left me babe.

(continued)

I'm still breathing,
But I'm not living anymore,
I don't go out now,
Yet I still walk through the door.
I just feel numb babe,
Even though my heart is sore,
Because you left me babe.

I look at photos,
Of how things used to be,
Of smiling faces,
With you right next to me,
And lovely places,
And the things we used to see,
Before you left me babe.

Still got your picture,
Pinned up upon my wall,
It's always been there,
I tell friends who come and call,
But the truth is,
I can't take it down at all,
Because I miss you.

And your new guy,
I met him yesterday.
He seems a nice guy,
What more can I now say,
I hope you're happy,
In every single way,
Even though,
You left me babe,
You left me babe,
You left me babe.

79.

SPRINGTIME.

How I love the woods in springtime,
Where all is new, with freshness all around,
The only place a man can really breathe,
The only song a voice can sing without a sound.

The woods are green right now,
All those barren snows of winter are dried,
Warm sunlight shines brightly through high branches,
To justly compliment the living countryside.

Ahead, I see a clearing on a hilltop,
Alive with flowers, so still and undisturbed,
Below, a dancing brook is proudly singing,
A song so clear, with honest noble words.

The scent of life is living all around me,
To feel so fresh, so cool, and really free,
Alive in harmony, with the innocence of springtime,
Sun-stained sleepy woodlands fall on me.

How I love the woods in springtime,
Where all is new, with freshness all around,
The only place a man can really breathe,
The only song a voice can sing without a sound.

80.

JUST FLY.

She glides,
Through a meadow green,
Her eyes,
Smile at what they've seen,
Her heart,
Skips a beat,
Each time that they meet,
As her arms,
Reach out for his touch,
She knows,
That he means so much,
To her,
As she flies into his arms,
And then,
She cries.

To him,
She has angel's wings,
Which bring,
All the special things,
The things,
That he dreams every day,
When she's so far away,
So,
He holds her tight,
And speaks,
Of his love tonight,
Each word,
Brings a tear from her eye,
As they,
Just fly.

81.

SHE.

She moves, like a breeze through a storm,
She weeps, as each new day is born,
She smiles, like a lost Mona Lisa,
She blooms, as the autumn leaves fall.

She is my life, she is my song,
She is my meaning, to love and belong,
She is my heart, she is my wealth,
She is my being, my waking, my sleeping,
My love and my strength.

What would I do, if she would go,
Could I survive then, the answer is no,
For she is my day, she is my night,
She is my dream, and my hope, and my needs,
And my heart in full flight.

She moves, like a breeze through a storm,
She weeps, as each new day is born,
She smiles, like a lost Mona Lisa,
She blooms, as the autumn leaves fall,
For she is she.

82.

YOU.

Are you a wonderful enigma,
Or a glorious cascade,
Are you a princess in a castle,
Or an angel heaven made,
Are you real or just a vision,
Or the song I need to sing,
Are you a wave upon the sand,
Or a dove that's on the wing.

Are they real and are they true,
These dreams I dream of you.

It is you who fills my heart,
And enchants my every prayer,
With your movement and your beauty,
No other can compare,
Like a fountain in a meadow,
Or a blossom newly kissed,
Or a hazy ghostly vision,
Rising slowly from the mists.

Are they real and are they true,
These dreams I dream of you.

(continued)

Are you the artists final brushstrokes,
Which create a great encore,
Or a waterfall at daybreak,
Like the visions I adore,
Or a glancing smile one evening,
Sent to take my breath away,
Or a sigh to fill my heart,
For another endless day.

Are they real and are they true,
These dreams I dream of you.

Are you a wonderful enigma,
Or a glorious cascade,
Are you a princess in a castle,
Or an angel heaven made,
Are you real or just a vision,
Or the song I need to sing,
Are you a wave upon the sand,
Or a dove that's on the wing.

Are they real and are they true,
These dreams I dream of you.

83.

WHAT IF.

What if, the sky was blue,
What if, the trees were green,
With all the flowers, in bloom,
No this is not, a dream.

What if I held, your hand,
Then gazed into, your eyes,
I think you'd, understand,
With you my heart, just flies.

What if I held, you close,
My fingers through, your hair,
Then gently kissed, your lips,
A love we both, can share.

What if, the sky was blue,
What if, the trees were green,
With all the flowers, in bloom,
No this is not, a dream.

84.

ANOTHER DAY.

Don't ask me if my life is normal,
Because I don't know what normal means,
All I know is my life was fine once,
Until you left me on my knees.

Don't ask me how I'm feeling,
When I'm left sitting on the floor,
You say you're sorry, but you found a new guy,
And you don't love me anymore.

I have no hopes, and I can't dream now,
I came in last in some big race,
I'm afraid to close my eyes,
For when I do I see your face.

People ask me, where have you gone,
I just smile and say, away,
But I still look out for your smile,
After all, tomorrow is another day.

85.

THE PAPER CINEMA.

The old lady gently and lovingly removes her favourite book from the case,
Elegantly and carefully placing it onto her highly polished reading desk.
She slowly sits, and a warm smile becomes apparent as she begins to read,
Her respect for every word is plain to see, as she runs her fingers over each line.
She doesn't look at the pages, she simply counts them as each page turns,
As she reads purely from memory, for her eyesight faded long ago.
Yet, the pleasure in her face, tells me that she reads this book very well,
And with more emotion than I could ever have imagined.

86.

STREET LIFE.

You see her walking through the city,
Her worldly goods all in one bag,
Dressed in several ragged layers,
Oh, she always looks so sad.

When it's hot she must be sweating,
But come the winter she is cold,
She ain't getting any younger,
This year she looks so old.

She speaks the words of thank you,
Her eyes say please help me,
As everyone walks past her,
Their choice is not to see.

Each day I give her my smile,
A little something for some food,
I never wish to walk on past her,
To blank her out would just be rude.

You see her walking through the city,
Her worldly goods all in one bag,
Dressed in several ragged layers,
Oh, she always looks so sad.

87.

AWAKENING.

Lean out of the window,
Taste the morning mist,
Let your wild hair ripple in the breeze.
Clear your sleepy eyes,
Stretch your tired arms,
Watch the cool breeze dance amid the trees.

Hear the tree birds sing,
Watch the brown leaves fall,
See the birds set out on their long flight,
As nature turns a page,
As autumn takes the stage,
Taste the morning mist and touch the light.

88.

THE PALLY IS CLOSED.

The blue carpet is worn by the dancing feet,
Tobacco stains the roof and walls,
Torn wallpaper sits where once sat a seat,
Through broken glass the outside calls.

A pigeon flies inside the roof,
Its wings click click and amplify,
A cobweb catches a glint of sun,
Sad, yet pleasing to the eye.

The old caretaker locks the door,
And pins up the sign ‘Closed for good’.
A little girl smiles as she reads the sign,
As she stands where the queues once stood.

89.

OLD LADY.

Sitting alone on a chair in a doorway,
Watching the world as the world passes by,
Smiling at strangers who move past her garden,
Not caring and not caring why.

She finds herself more and more in the doorway,
And she looks so alone in her place on her chair,
Feeling sad when she thinks no one's watching,
Yet smiling at once, once they're there.

Her old flowered dress sits well in the sunlight,
Her grey thinning hair shows her age,
In her world the people who walk past are actors,
As her life is a series of plays.

At dusk, she turns from the street and the doorway,
And retires, as she waits for the sun,
She rests and reflects on her day in the doorway,
Then she dreams of the new day to come.

POETIC IMAGES.

Like the sails upon a windmill,
Or a forests sweet perfume,
A sleigh ride in a snowfall,
Or a meadow in full bloom.
Raindrops in the morning,
Casting ripples on a lake,
A summers golden sunset
Catching every breath I take.
Or the waves upon the sea,
Painting pictures just for me.

Like a dove upon the wing,
Or a nightingale's sweet call,
A pleasant summer breeze,
Or the autumn leaves that fall.
The poetry of colours,
Painting rainbows in the sky,
A clear and starlit evening,
Compelling me to sigh.
Or the waves upon the sea,
Painting pictures just for me.

Like the sails upon a windmill,
Or a forests sweet perfume,
A sleigh ride in a snowfall,
Or a meadow in full bloom.
Raindrops in the morning,
Casting ripples on a lake,
A summers golden sunset,
Catching every breath I take.
Or the waves upon the sea,
Painting pictures just for me.

91.

THE AVENUE.

Through netted curtains another day begins to flow
before its weary fade into night.
Shadows rise to turn and flow,
Avenue trees drip wet with rain,
Collectively caught in a shower amid a day of blazing sun.
This same sun dries the pavement once more,
To aid a haze which fills the avenue with steamy mists.
The avenue basks in ghostly visions.

Tree birds fly down to scour the soil for insects loosened by the rain.
They feed and drink until the dusk,
Then fly back to their skies again.

The darkness creeps in slowly first,
But once around it closes fast,
It brings a chill with stars and moon,
Then hides the truth of days long past.

92.

ALONE AGAIN.

I don't think,
That my heart, is the first to feel heavy.
I don't think,
It's the first, to cry.
Maybe I am,
The first, to shed tears over you,
Because you're gone,
And I don't, understand why.

Why did you say, each day,
That you loved me.
Why did you sigh, each night,
At my touch.
Why did you say, each day,
That you're mine.
And why,
Did you smile, so much.

For now,
My lonely heart, is broken,
For now,
My weeping eyes, won't dry.
Wet pillows,
Reveal, the true story,
Ever since,
The day you said, goodbye.

(continued)

At the start,
When our love, was perfect.
You promised,
Love was here, to stay.
But this evening, as I gaze,
To the streets, far below,
I know,
That your love's, flown away.

I don't think
That my heart, is the first to feel heavy.
I don't think,
It's the first, to cry.
Maybe I am,
The first, to shed tears over you,
Because you're gone,
And I don't, understand why.

93.

THE GHOST OF BARLEEZE.

Do you know of the ghost of Barleeze,
He walks the hills and screams from the trees.
His flute plays music wherever he roams,
Haunting sounds which chill to the bones.

Each village, each town, are afraid of his name,
His cold lifeless music will drive you insane.
For evil follows each step that he takes,
He captures a soul with each tune he makes.

Wherever he walks you see lightning strike,
As loud thunder roars deep into the night.
Folk fall to their knees, and pray to the skies,
For they know on this night another soul dies.

Do you know of the ghost of Barleeze,
He walks the hills and screams from the trees.
His flute plays music wherever he roams,
Haunting sounds which chill to the bones.

94.

THE DOG THAT NEVER WAS.

You hear him howling late at night,
All through the blackened fog,
Sometimes he cries in torment,
But no one sees that dog.

His legend goes back many years,
To the time of long before,
Yet his crying stays forever,
As he roams the hills once more.

No one knows of whence he came,
Nor his mission, nor his cause,
Still the village lives in fear,
Of the dog that never was.

95.

HERSHWHIN COOP.

We all went on the picnic,
Her and me and he and they.
We ate and talked and drank and laughed,
And ate and talked away.

We sat on top of blankets,
And waved and winced and smiled,
Gracefully her wine was spilled,
His lip curled as a child.

She uttered something tasteless,
We changed the subject far,
He relaxed and she relaxed,
I lit a small cigar.

I scanned the sporting pages,
She varnished her nails red,
He sucked a piece of common grass,
The sun is hot they said.

Oh, what a peaceful Sunday,
With company good and free,
With little Hershwhin Coop the dog,
And he and her and they and me.

96.

THE CITY.

Cars and buses choke the roads,
Hurried anxious people squabble,
Housewives move in darting hoards,
City gents move at the double.

Lights say, stop, or go, or wait,
Every second shop says sale,
Buskers who are hard to rate,
Crowded pubs and putrid ale.

Elderly drunks sit sprawled and dirty,
Raincoat men sell damaged goods,
Courts that judge the good and guilty,
Chemists who sell health with drugs.

Yellow perils called traffic wardens,
Boys in blue in bobby cars,
Theatre, cinema, public gardens,
Bottles, boxes, tins and jars.

Hungry merchants who, never lie,
Swindle people from afar,
Still, we go to the city,
Why? What for?

97.

PINSTRIPE PUPPET.

I watch him promptly stride his stroll,
Head up straight and shoulders back,
Rigid stature, measured stride,
Black brolly, tie, and bowler hat.

The elderly gentleman shows his pace,
His proud nose plainly pointing up,
No fluff nor hair are on his cloth,
Uniformed, personal, pinstripe suit.

A living advert of his class,
A portrait of the city gent,
A pinstripe puppet out to grass,
Stamped and sealed in retirement.

LOVING YOU.

One day you walked away,
And left me,
You thought that you'd found,
Someone new.
I was upset and lonely,
It was hard to face,
Or even see a life,
Without you.

But now you've returned,
To say sorry,
Your tears tell me,
That you're sincere.
So, as I dry your eyes,
Please don't worry,
The main thing for me,
Is you're here.

I can feel the way,
You hold me,
I just know that you need to be,
Back in my arms,
As I stroke your soft hair,
Perfume fills the air,
Along with lost,
Returned, charms.

(continued)

I don’t need to know,
Why you left me,
I don’t really care,
Where you’ve been,
All I know is you’re back,
In my arms once again,
So, once more,
I’m living the dream.

99.

MERRY CHRISTMAS.

It's Christmas eve, and gently snowing,
The ground is crisp, and clean and white,
I hear some children, singing carols,
As sleigh bells jingle, through the night.

The snowman stands, in all his splendour,
Top hat, a smile, and carrot nose,
Smiling faces, of young children,
Even though, a cold wind blows.

Fairy lights, shine from the parlour,
Candy sticks, hang from the tree,
Tinsel glistens, in the firelight,
Shining colours, dancing free.

Chestnut's roasting, on the fire,
Cheesy snacks, and hot mull wine,
Stolen kisses, under mistletoe,
End the evening, with a smile.

It's Christmas eve, and gently snowing,
The ground is crisp, and clean and white,
I hear some children, singing carols,
As sleigh bells jingle, through the night.

100.

MY SECRET VALENTINE.

From this nervous stranger,
Whose words are dark or lost,
I delve into my heart,
To find the words I must.

Are you a princess in a forest,
Or a glorious cascade,
Are you the snows upon a mountain,
Or an angel heaven made.
Are you smiles or are you laughter,
Or a vision I once seen,
Are you grace and are you beauty,
Or the dream I dare to dream.

Are you warm and are you true,
For these things I see in you.

I'll be your knight upon white charger,
Colours flying in the breeze,
I'll guard your beauty and your honour,
Bringing foes upon their knees.
I'll never ask you any questions,
Never tell you any lies,
All I pray is for one kiss,
And to gaze into your eyes.

Are you warm and are you true,
For these things I see in you.

(continued)

Are you a princess in a forest,
Or a glorious cascade,
Are you the snows upon a mountain,
Or an angel heaven made.
Are you smiles or are you laughter,
Or a vision I once seen,
Are you grace and are you beauty,
Or the dream I dare to dream.

Are you warm and are you true,
For these things I see in you.

101.

HAPPY STREET.

I’m walking down a happy street,
Smiling at the people walking by.
The sun is shining, all is well,
It feels so good,
With you right by my side.

You were lost, but now you’re back,
Both together, back where we belong.
Smiling faces, happy eyes,
Underneath the bright blue skies,
Walking in the sun where we belong.

With music playing in my head,
When all’s been done and all’s been said,
It’s really nice to hear, a happy song.
The mood is bright, I’m feeling good,
It feels so right, I know it can’t be wrong.

I’m walking down a happy street,
Smiling at the people walking by.
The sun is shining, all is well,
It feels so good,
With you right by my side.

102.

DREAMY RAINBOW LAND.

Floating down a river on a giant rubber duck,
With fairy-tale cast steamboats drifting by.
The air smells just like homemade jam,
And cartoon men wave from the sky.

The trees have blooms of chocolate drops,
The grass has gentle golden hairs,
There's clouds of fluffy ice cream dabs,
And crowds of cuddly teddy bears.

Yet only children visit here,
As adults are too old,
And anyway, when they're about,
You must do as you're told.

For this is dreamy rainbow land,
Mother nature's secret park,
Where folk are friendly all the time,
And little creatures talk.

To visit dreamy rainbow land,
Is easy when you're young,
Just lay down you head, and close your eyes,
And dream of having fun.

103.

NIGHT OF DAY.

In a world of black and white,
You turned my sunny days back into night.
All the trees have turned to grey,
Since you took your love away,
All the trees have turned to grey.

Dark flowers have no perfume,
In this chilling winter month of June.
All the river boats stand still,
No rivers flow nor never will,
In a world of black and white.

And all the stars fell from the sky,
As I watched the final rainbow die.
With the sun masked by a cloud,
As the thunder roared out loud,
In a world of black and white.

Cold driving rain upon my face,
In this dark and very empty place.
A lovers wish which shone so bright,
Until you sent me with no light,
To a world of black and white.

In a world of black and white,
You turned my sunny days back into night.
All the trees have turned to grey,
Since you took your love away,
All the trees have turned to grey.

104.

SUMMER ROMANCE.

With the sun's rays shining down upon me,
Dreaming sweetly as the heat turns up slowly,
Just basking in the sounds of the sea,
With you lying right next to me.

Arms reaching out to hold tight,
Dancing fingers stroke my face in the sunlight,
Whispered tender words so sweet and so right,
As our two beating hearts take flight.

Soft kisses in the warm breeze,
Blue eyes you use to flatter and tease me,
Red lips that are just asking with ease,
Hold me tight and kiss me please.

With the sun's rays shining down upon me,
Dreaming sweetly as the heat turns up slowly,
Just basking in the sounds of the sea,
With you lying right next to me.

105.

LIVING IN A DREAM.

Don't go crying, in the rain please,
Things are not the way they seem.
I still love you, just as much babe,
But we are living in a dream.

Life is true girl, and it's tough girl,
And some things, aren't meant to be.
We both have loved ones, to protect girl,
And their eyes won't let them see.

So, don't go crying, in the rain please,
Things are not the way they seem.
I still love you, just as much babe,
But we are living in a dream.

We know it's time now, to say goodbye now,
We need to walk our separate ways.
We have sweet memories, for all time girl,
Of starlit nights, and summer days.

So, don't go crying, in the rain please,
Things are not the way they seem.
I still love you, just as much babe,
But we've been living in a dream.

MY YOUNG FRIEND.

I was on a holiday in Europe,
Relaxing away my days,
Reading books, and drinking coffee,
In a small café.
Most every morning,
Was spent this way.

After a few days,
A young lady would join me daily.
We spoke of many things,
Her passion was Royal history,
And the world of kings.

Her broken English sounded charming,
For Russian I can't speak.
We'd built up one special friendship,
By the second week.

On my last day,
She handed me an envelope,
Saying 'read it once you're home'.
Inside there was an old photo of her,
And I was overcome.

For the photograph,
Showed that she was of royal blood,
A daughter of the Tsar.
But this photograph of Anastasia,
Was dated,
One hundred years before.

107.

FLOWERS TO A FALLEN FRIEND.

I never wanted to believe it could be true,
I never wanted to believe it could be you.
Through all the dark days, the days of pain,
Those days of running down dark alleys in the rain.

But I can see now, the reasons why,
And I can feel now, a need to cry.

They held your sister with a gun against her head,
They wrote the script for you to say the things you said.
You were a traitor, or so I thought,
I never stopped to think of loyalties you taught.

So, now I stand here, with flowers in hand,
Just praying, you'll understand.

I never wanted to believe it could be true,
I never wanted to believe it could be you.
Through all the dark days, the days of pain,
Those days of running down dark alleys in the rain.

108.

SLEEPY VALENTINE.

Oh, my sleepy valentine,
With perfume dancing in your hair,
In what dreams is it that you walk,
Please take my hand and lead me there.

Rest, my sleepy valentine,
As I watch over you.
No harm will spoil your fantasy,
So, drift till morning dew.
Your closed eyes mask a starlit sky,
As in your dreams you stay,
Happy dreams which yield a sigh,
To steal my heart away.
So, rest my sleepy valentine,
Cascade into the night,
For as I rest your hand in mine,
I feel our hearts take flight.
Soaring high above the clouds,
Then flying to the stars,
All at once we are as one,
The way it always was.

Shh, don't stir my sleepy valentine,
For this is meant to be,
With you just resting in my arms,
So beautiful to see.

109.

THE OLD DANCER.

Dancing to the music of the songs of long ago,
The old girl has the movement,
Though her timing's rather slow.
She pretends she holds a partner,
Who can whisk her round the floor,
But her partner is a figment,
Who once held her years before.

Still, she dances, and she dances, and she dances,
Like a princess on the clouds inside her mind,
And her poise is strong with purpose,
As she struts around in style.
She could be a ballerina or a smouldering flamenco,
She could twirl or tap or samba,
There's no rules to where she'd go.

So, she dances, and she dances, and she dances,
Like a princess on the clouds inside her mind,
And her poise is strong with purpose,
As she struts around in style.
As her memories bring smiling lips,
And a look that's quite sublime,
As she dances, and she dances,
And she dances back in time.

110.

ALL ALONE AT CHRISTMAS.

All alone at Christmas,
So, it's just another day.
All alone at Christmas,
With loved ones gone away.

Where did all the good times go,
As the long cold years pass by.
I wonder where the people went,
As I stare at an empty sky.

Never got a card this year,
For the first time in my life.
No one ever visits me,
Just to see if I'm alive.

I often look at my telephone,
But I never hear it ring.
I cannot force a smile these days,
And I've forgotten how to sing.

No decorations up once more,
Never bothered with a tree.
I'm only left with memories,
Of how things used to be.

All alone at Christmas,
So, it's just another day.
I'm all alone at Christmas,
With loved ones gone away.

111.

THE ONLY GIRL FOR ME.

You know you are the only girl for me,
And right here, is the place you need to be.
So, stop your ways of running all around,
That what you seek, you've already found.

The grass is no more greener over there,
And you will find no better, anywhere.
So, settle down and open your eyes,
For I'm sure one day you'll realise.

I'm the safest bet you'll ever make,
Can't you feel my love, for heaven's sake.
Don't search for a love which can't be true,
When it's standing here in front of you.

I pray one day you'll notice me,
Gaze into my eyes and you'll plainly see.
The love you're seeking every day,
Has never been so far away.

You know you are the only girl for me,
And right here, is the place you need to be.

112.

DANCING IN THE DARK.

The memories of you,
Seem untrue,
You feel a million miles away.
I'm left in a trance,
As your smile and your glance,
Haunt me every day.

I have walked with you,
Down this avenue,
Come sun, or snow, or rain.
Now I'm walking alone,
Wherever I roam,
And it doesn't feel the same.

A last kiss on my cheek,
As you left for a week,
But you never did return.
I never did any wrong,
I just fell for your charm,
But you left me here to burn.

My memories of you,
Seem so untrue,
You feel a million miles away.
I'm left in a trance,
As your smile and your glance,
Haunt me every day.

113.

ONCE AGAIN.

Autumn is here once again,
As I walk in the rain,
How, I feel it.
Golden leaves, down on the ground,
Make a rustling sound,
Can't you, hear it.

Right here, on this windy day,
Old hopes, are all blown way,
Still, I daydream through the rain,
Once again.

Picturing your face in the leaves,
As I gaze through the trees,
Can't you see me.
Whispering your name from my heart,
Since we drifted apart,
Can't you hear me.

An autumn day, spent alone,
Knowing, that you are the one,
You are the one for me,
Can't you see.

I wish that you were here once again,
As I walk in the rain,
Without you.
I wish that you were holding my hand,
So, I could stand,
Beside you.

Right here, on this windy day,
Old hopes, are all blown away,
As I daydream through the rain,
Once again.

114.

LADY.

Lady,
you'd never know at all,
This way that I feel,
These feelings are real,
It's hard to conceal,
That I love you.

Lady,
Although, we've both been friends,
For many years,
Our friendship hides tears,
Behind all the years,
That I've loved you.

Lady,
Each time I meet with you,
I breathe once more,
It gives me more time,
To adore you.

Lady,
This love that I feel, is so very real,
I know it is true,
But after hiding each day,
I just can't find a way,
To say...
I love you.

115.

A TEXT GOODBYE.

I'm walking down a railway track,
Looking ahead, no looking back, Oh no.
A new life lies ahead of me,
I'll see the things I need to see,
I'll be in places I should be,
And you should never follow me, Oh no.

I'm on my way, seeking tomorrow,
To reach my dreams, beg, steal, or borrow.
I've tried your way, it brings me sorrow,
Now I need to walk away and start again.

I'm sure you loved me, and I loved you too,
I loved your ways, the things that you to do.
But different dreams, made me feel blue,
So, it's time to walk away, and start again.

I'm walking down a railway track,
Looking ahead, no looking back, Oh no.
A new life lies ahead of me,
I'll see the things I need to see,
I'll be in places I should be,
And you should never follow me.

116.

VELVET DREAMS.

Floating in a velvet dream,
Reflecting on the things I feel,
As I live out a lover's dream,
With you.

All you do, the things you say,
The way you kiss me every day,
And how you smile that special way,
You do.

I'll never understand quite why,
This feeling like I need to fly,
I feel it more as time goes by,
With you.

And any day you're far from me,
No matter where that place may be,
I close my eyes and all I see,
Is you.

Floating in a velvet dream,
Reflecting on the things I feel,
As I live out a lover's dream,
With you.

117.

LOVES EMBERS.

As I walk a morning forest,
In the autumn of the year,
I am left with distant memories,
Of you, and how things were.
Like how we met in springtime,
And the dreams we dared to dream,
With life just gently turning,
As the spokes upon a wheel.
Then holding hands so tight,
In the romance of the night.

As springtime turned to summer,
Summer heat, and summer love,
Forever growing closer,
As we gazed at stars above.
Love which glistened from the heavens,
As the moonlight lit your eyes,
With our dreams just floating lightly,
As they washed across the skies.
Like a sonnet in full cry,
Beneath our dreams across the sky.

Now with autumn you have left me,
I can't get you out my head,
Where did things go oh so wrong,
Was it something that I said.

They say that life is strange,
And sometimes not too fair,
As I watch the autumn leaves,
Turn to, the colour of your hair.

118.

SEA OF LOVE.

The morning sky fills up my eyes,
With coloured rays that hypnotise,
Touching all the clouds which may appear,
Like a dream that seems so far yet near.
As silk reflections sit upon a sea of calm,
With all its charm,
As I just stand, and wonder.

I see some shadows far away,
Breaking through the silk to play,
Dancing gently on a morning breeze,
Then drifting slowly up, to glide with ease.
Each shadow holds a wish of better things,
Upon its wings,
As I just stand, and wonder.

I ask which shadow holds my name,
Or are they somehow all the same,
Turning slowly as they paint the sky,
Gazing at them, as I see them fly.
They whisper that my dreams may all come true,
My dreams of you,
But I just stand, and wonder.

119.

WHISPERED STARLIGHT.

Daylight is fading,
Waving in the evening,
Sunlight dying,
As the stars start flying.

Moonbeams show a pathway,
To a place where children's minds play.
I look up to see dreams flying high,
As my heart is lost,
To visions of the sky.

Holding your hand,
Walking on the soft sand,
Smiling faces,
Warm and soft embraces.

Swaying here beside you,
As we dance away the night through,
Hearing all your whispered words of love,
While gazing, at the heavens high above.

Moonbeams show a pathway,
To a place where children's minds play.
I look up to see dreams flying high,
As my heart is lost to you,
And visions of the sky.

120.

DECLARATION OF LOVE.

Do I need to tell you, I adore you,
Do I need to say you're part of me,
Don't you know I love you so,
I thought it must be plain to see.

Don't you feel, that when I'm with you,
All my troubles fade away,
Can't you sense I'm dreaming of you,
Every moment, night and day.

Can't you see, my face light up,
Each time that you move closer still,
Can't you feel the things you should,
The things I feel, and always will.

Do I need to say, I love you,
Can't you feel it deep inside,
Don't you feel the way I feel,
A feeling which I cannot hide.

Do I need to tell you, I adore you,
Do I need to say you're part of me,
Don't you know I love you so,
I thought it must be plain to see.

121.

DREAMS.

Why do I dream of you again,
Never knowing where or when,
We may meet once more.

How can I sense your perfume,
In this dark and empty room,
A room you've never been before.

On a lonely chilly evening,
Where the moonlight is hidden away,
I softly whisper, I love you,
In a hope you will hear me one day.

I never asked your name,
I don't know where you're from,
But when you left you took my heart away.

So, I'll stay here in this small room,
Hoping you may find me soon,
Then I'll know a special love may bloom.

Why do I dream of you again,
Never knowing where or when,
We may meet once more.

122.

FREESCAPE.

Did you ever want to stand up tall and see,
The beauty which surrounds us,
From the heavens far and wide,
To a snowcapped misty mountain,
Silhouetted either side,
With a rollercoaster landscape free to ride.

Did you ever want to hide away,
In a secret forest,
High up in the hills,
Where all the air is pure,
And nature spreads her wings,
Where all our problems fade to lesser things.

Did you ever want to be alone,
Just living in the moment,
With all those troubles gone,
Soaking up the wonder,
Of where we all came from,
And not caring if it's right or if it's wrong.

Did you ever want to stand up tall and see,
The beauty which surrounds us,
From the heavens far and wide,
To a snowcapped misty mountain,
Silhouetted either side,
With a rollercoaster landscape free to ride.

123.

AHA.

Case in hand on an escalator,
I’m going away but you say you’ll see me later,
Aha.

I thought I knew you, but I know I don’t,
You said you will, but I know you won’t,
Aha.

Our sweet romance was two weeks long,
You say that you’ll visit once I’m gone,
Aha.

But I could see it in your eyes,
And all at once I realized I’m wrong,
Aha.

I know that was our last goodbye,
I knew it when I turned to see you cry,
Aha.

So, now my heart is feeling low,
I know it’s over, and I have to go,
Aha.

Case in hand on an escalator,
I’m going away but you say you’ll see me later,
Aha.

I know that was our last goodbye,
I knew it when I turned to see you cry.

124.

SHIFTING SANDS.

I try to walk on shifting sands,
My feet don't work so I clinch my hands,
And say,
I'm needing you to stand by me,
But your closed eyes just will not see,
The way.

I loved you every day and night,
But all you did was shout and fight,
With me.
And now I'm sinking in the sand,
But you won't lend a helping hand,
To me.

I don't know what I need to do,
All I know is I need you,
Today.
But as I try to talk with you,
You look at me with eyes of blue,
And say…
Your love for me has been and gone,
And everything feels very wrong,
Tonight.
So now you're walking out the door,
A thing you said you'd do,
When it felt right.

(continued)

I try to walk on shifting sands,
My feet don’t work so I clench my hands,
And say.
I’m needing you to stand by me,
But you just shake your head and,
Walk away.

I loved you every day and night,
But all you did was shout and fight,
With me.
And now I’m sinking in the sand,
But you won’t lend a helping hand,
To me.

125.

SEASONS.

In January love was new,
We never noticed the cutting winds,
As remnants of winter still chilled the frozen ground.
A month of endless smiles and miles and miles,
Of walks hand in hand to lead us into springtime.
A blustery spring, but warmer than some,
With the odd clear day of blazing sun.
The day of the daffodil came soon,
As meadows reflected an early bloom.
Summer was warm and intense,
As warm as the skies above.
We soared through summer on a wave of love.
Autumn turned bitter as our romance was tested,
A time of long conversations,
With much time invested.
A bitter bleak winter,
As warm love turned cold,
Sad tears as love died,
As our new love grew old.

ALL DONE.
Thanks for reading.
I think I'll have a nap now.
A. A. HEDLEY.

Want to know more about the author?
Visit his book page online, it's followed by thousands.
It's called 'About my detective novels and more'
@MyNewNoveljolantasRevenge

Printed in Great Britain
by Amazon